Printer in the United States of America.
First Printing, 2021
**ISBN:** 9798791414731

Independently Published

## DEDICATED TO

The first person in my life to see that I would one day
become a published author. I only needed to dig deep
and find the strength to share my stories.

She was right.

For Ms. Jill Wilkins- where all my stories began.

"Success is failure turned inside out.
The silver tint of the clouds of doubt,
And you never can tell how close you are,
It may be near when it seems so far,
So stick to the fight when you're hardest hit.
It's when things seem worst that you must not quit."

-Edgar A. Guest, *Don't Quit*

# IZZIE GOES DIGGING

## A STORY OF RESILIENCE

by Madi Franquiz

**Everyone knows that dwarfs love shiny things.**

**They love gems**
**and metal**
**and all that blings.**

**But the one thing they love the most is gold.**
**For this reason, dwarfs learn to dig, I'm told.**

**The dwarfs begin digging
when they are young**

**working all day
until their ax is hung.**

**They shovel the dirt
searching for treasure.
All day they look
for what brings them pleasure.**

**After years of working hard underground,**

the dwarfs are very short

and stout

and round.

While all dwarfs were strong
and acted very gruff,

our girl Izzie was slight, tender,
and not rough.

Yet though she was small
and not very tall,
she always gave more effort
than them all.

Out of all the dwarfs,
even the tallest,

everyone knew Izzie
worked the longest.

Every day,
she would work hard all alone

**and crash into bed when she made it home.**

After all the digging
with her hands,

you would think she would
have all the gold in the land.

But Izzie had a big problem,
you see.

She had emeralds, sapphires, and rubies.

But she had yet to find any gold,

and every dwarf knows
gold's the best to hold.

While many thought Izzie's hard work was cool,
others were bullies and were very cruel.

They would meanly call her Izzie, the small,
and mock her for not finding gold at all.

**Yet one thing about Izzie was for sure:**

she wasn't a quitter,
she would endure.

Everyday she worked harder than before.
She was determined to always do more.

She would find gems of every shape and size,
but she kept looking for gold- the true prize.

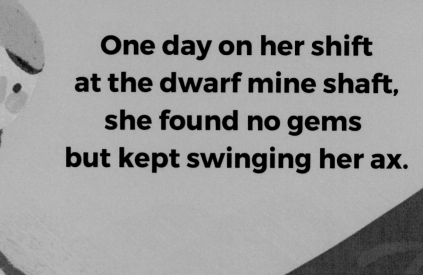

One day on her shift
at the dwarf mine shaft,
she found no gems
but kept swinging her ax.

Today she was determined to strike gold.
She'd do what it took.
She'd be brave and bold.

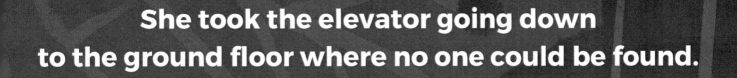

She took the elevator going down
to the ground floor where no one could be found.

No one had been down on this floor in years.

It was dark
and damp
and filled her with fear.

Pushing past her fear that seemed ever so big,
she took a deep breath and began to dig.

For what felt like a century, Izzie dug
'til her arms hurt and were covered with bugs.

From her boots to her helmet to her shirt
every part of her was covered in dirt.

**Frustrated, Izzie thought about leaving
but she pushed through and kept persevering.**

**She thrust in her shovel time and again
and was surrounded by dirt in the end.**

She looked around and said with a deep sigh.
"Ok. I'll give it one last try."

She dug her shovel in the ground once more,
and out came a sound she'd not heard before.

She had hit many gems lining the hall,
but this sound was different,
unlike them all.

She picked up her ax and swung hard once more.
The same loud DING echoed across the floor.

Izzie threw down her ax,
grabbed her shovel,
and began to dig
through piles of rubble.

She waited to hear a similar sound.
At last, she hit something solid and round.

**Concerned she may have hurt what she had found
she dug with her hands as she knelt on the ground.**

She dug until dirt was under her nails
when suddenly something shone bright and pale.

It glittered and blinded her with its light,
and from the dirt she pulled a gem so bright.

Izzie handed the gem to her Master
thinking it was a complete disaster

He gasped so loud it echoed underground,
and asked,
"Izzie, do you know what you've found!?"

Confused, Izzie shook her head in reply
and the master exclaimed with a loud cry,
"This is a diamond, the rarest gem of all!

It's more valuable than all the gold
that lines the Great Hall!"

Before their master had finished speaking,
the dwarfs raced below with joyous singing

to see the cavern
where Izzie had found
the beautiful gem
with which she was crowned.

All the dwarfs began to dig,
and surprise!
There were piles of shiny rocks inside.

The truth is that Izzie had always found
gems in her kingdom that were all around.

All of her rubies, emeralds, and more
glittered on their ceilings, fountains, and floors,
but the diamond was the best gem of all,
found only because of Izzie, the small.

IZZIE'S DIAMOND MINE

Now their kingdom had found a great treasure
which changed the lives of the dwarfs forever.

The cavern was named, "Izzie's Diamond Mine,"
where they found both diamonds and gold that shine.

For all her hard work, this was her reward:

She was named leader of the Diamond Floor.

**When the going got tough, she didn't quit.**
**And that, dear friends, is what we call grit.**
**And Izzie, the small, was the queen of it.**

# MEET MADI

## About the Author

Having experienced poverty and hardship at an early age, Madi knows exactly how difficult it can be to overcome challenges. While attending a Title One school in 2nd Grade, Madi found it hard to dream big dreams when she didn't know where her next meal was coming from or when she would have to move again.

Sixteen years later, Madi is an author, an internationally recognized public speaker, and the founder of a women's empowerment organization called Becoming 31. Additionally, Madi works as an impassioned advocate for all children through the Miss America Organization. Through her curriculum and various resources, Madi seeks to equip the next generation with the foundational five traits that help everyone become better.

Her hope is that this book will empower parents to have conversations with their children about resilience, failure, and overcoming hardships. She firmly believes that conversations like these will equip the next generation to become all they were created to be.

# MEET KELLY

## About the Editor

Kelly has always had a passion for stories and believes that words hold tremendous weight as they have the potential to change children's lives.

For most children, reading is a challenging thing to learn, and it was no different for Kelly. It was not until she discovered that her love of stories, imagination, and adventure could be satisfied through books that she fell in love with reading. From that moment onward, she could never be found without a book.

Her hope is that this book will inspire a love for stories and reading in children, similar to her own, while teaching them valuable life lessons about hard work and perseverance.

Izzie will be back for more adventures in
*The Realm of Becoming* Series.

Made in the USA
Columbia, SC
12 February 2023

11998207R00027